The Christmas Knight

Jane Louise Curry

illustrated by DyAnne DiSalvo-Ryan

Margaret K. McElderry Books
New York

Maxwell Macmillan Canada
Toronto

Maxwell Macmillan International
New York   Oxford   Singapore   Sydney

for Joshua
J.L.C.

for my agent
Jane L. Feder
with blessings at Christmas and always
D.D.R.

TEXT COPYRIGHT © 1993 BY JANE LOUISE CURRY
ILLUSTRATIONS COPYRIGHT © 1993 BY DYANNE DISALVO-RYAN

Margaret K. McElderry Books   Maxwell Macmillan Canada, Inc.
Macmillan Publishing Company   1200 Eglinton Avenue East
866 Third Avenue   Suite 200
New York, NY 10022   Don Mills, Ontario M3C 3N1

Macmillan Publishing Company is part of the Maxwell Communication
Group of Companies.

FIRST EDITION

Printed in Hong Kong by South China Printing Company (1988) Ltd.
10 9 8 7 6 5 4 3 2 1
The text of this book is set in Trajanus.
The illustrations are rendered in watercolors and pencil on handmade
watercolor paper.

Library of Congress Cataloging-in-Publication Data
Curry, Jane Louise.
   The Christmas knight / Jane Louise Curry ; illustrated by DyAnne
DiSalvo-Ryan. — 1st ed.
      p.   cm.
   Summary: An impoverished knight finds a miracle when his cherry
tree blooms on Christmas Day, but greedy servants get in his way
when he tries to take the fruit to the King.
   ISBN 0-689-50572-8
   [1. Folklore—England.   2. Knights and knighthood—Folklore.]
I. DiSalvo-Ryan, DyAnne, ill.   II. Title.
PZ8.1.C97Ch   1993   [398.2]—dc20   92-2277

Retold from a tale in a fifteenth-century manuscript
in the Advocates Library in Edinburgh, Scotland.

Before the days of King Arthur, in the time when his father, Uther, was king, there lived a knight named Cleges, who loved a good fight and a merry song. In all the land no knight was braver or richer or kinder. Good Sir Cleges housed the homeless. He fed the foodless. He helped the hapless. And merry Dame Clarys, his wife, was as good and goodly as he.

Each year at Christmas Sir Cleges and Dame Clarys gave a feast almost as fine and festive as the king's own banquet at Caerleon. Knights and ladies came, friars and farmers, washerwomen and wayfarers. Everyone was invited. Not a soul stayed home.

Each year minstrels and musicians came, too. They ate and sang and harped and piped from noon until night. When the feasting at last was finished, Sir Cleges paid them with gold rings and rich robes, and sent them on their way.

For ten happy Christmases Sir Cleges held his feast. But in the eleventh year, to his surprise, he found his money boxes empty.

"This will never do!" the good knight said to Dame Clarys. So they mortgaged their farms, and with the borrowed gold, they had ten more years as joyful as the ten that had gone before.

Alas, the twentieth year passed and their mortgage fell due, but they had no money to settle the debt. So Good Sir Cleges and Dame Clarys, to pay what they owed, sold their castle and lands. All they could keep for themselves and their sons was one small farm with one stony field and one bony cow.

Once Sir Cleges was poor, his fine neighbors turned up their noses when they met him in town. His men-at-arms and his servants were ashamed to serve so threadbare a master, so by ones and by twos they left him. Poor Sir Cleges's heart was half broken, and Dame Clarys sighed to see him so sad.

By and by, King Uther came to visit his castle at Cardiff and proclaimed a great feast there for Christmas Day. His messengers carried the news to the fine folk far and wide. None came to invite Sir Cleges and Dame Clarys, though, for the king had heard no word of them all that long year and more.

On the day before Christmas, Sir Cleges was at work in his barnyard when he heard from far-off Cardiff Castle the king's musicians practicing tunes.

He sighed a great sigh. "Oh, woe is me! If I were not poor, I, too, could spread good Christmas cheer tomorrow."

Dame Clarys heard and ran to Sir Cleges to kiss him. "Do not be downhearted, dear husband," said she. "On Christmas Eve we should honor the Christ Child with cheerful hearts."

"And indeed we shall," he said. So they went in to their supper of soup and bread, and made merry.

On Christmas Day in the morning Sir Cleges went out into the garden and knelt in the snow under a bare cherry tree to bow his head and pray.

"I thank you, sweet Christ Child, that I am poor," he said. "For when I was rich I was proud. I loved the praise my good deeds earned near as much as I loved doing good."

No sooner did the good knight say, "Amen," than a branch from the cherry tree dropped on his head.

"Ow!" cried Sir Cleges. And then he cried, "Oh!"

For the branch that should have been bare bore green leaves and bright red cherries!

"A marvel! Come see!" Sir Cleges called to Dame Clarys. "A marvel!"

Dame Clarys tasted the cherries and found them sweet as summer sunshine. She clapped her hands in wonder. "'Tis a marvel indeed, good husband. A Christmas gift from God! I shall pick them all, and you shall carry them to the king."

And so they did. Sir Cleges took up his staff and led the way to Cardiff, and his elder son walked behind with the basket of cherries. Dame Clarys bade them both Godspeed.

At Cardiff Castle, the porter at the gate would not allow Sir Cleges and his son to pass, for he saw only their shabby cloaks and well-worn boots.

"Stop, you raggedy rascals!" he roared. "You cannot pass. Go stand in the beggars' row where you belong, or I must call the guard."

"But I carry a gift from God to the king," said Sir Cleges, and he showed the porter the wonderful cherries.

The porter stared, then grinned a greedy grin. "Midwinter cherries! The king is sure to give you good thanks. If I let you pass, will you promise me a third of whatever he pays you?"

Sir Cleges argued, but what could he do? So he and his son passed into the castle. The usher who stood at the door of the king's great hall struck the stone floor with his staff when he spied them.

"Stop! You frowzy fellows have no business here. Begone before I call the guard!"

"But I bear a gift from God to the king," Sir Cleges explained, and he showed him the basket of cherries.

"Ah! A fair gift indeed." The usher smiled a sly smile. "The king will surely reward the giver of so fine a gift. Of course you may go in—if you will pledge me a third part of the gift he grants you."

Sir Cleges was dismayed, but what could he do?

In the great hall a throng of fine folk crowded the benches below the king's high table. But King Uther's splendid steward barred Sir Cleges's way with his golden rod.

"For shame, man! How dare you enter the king's great hall in workaday clothes?"

"Because I bear a gift from God to the king," said Sir Cleges, and he bade his son uncover the basket.

"A kingly gift in truth!" the steward exclaimed. A guileful gleam lit his eye. "Good sir, you are welcome to the feast—if first you avow me a third part of any reward King Uther may award you."

Poor Sir Cleges sighed, but what could he do? "At least," said he to his son, "we will have a good meal for our trouble."

When Sir Cleges's turn came to present his gift to King Uther, the king threw up his hands in amazement and called for all in the hall to see.

"Here is a winter wonder indeed—summer's cherries on Christmas Day! Good thanks to you, friend farmer. Sit you down at our feast and eat."

After the roast pig and the pies and the pudding, King Uther ate a whole bowl of the wonderful cherries. Then he called Sir Cleges from his place at the table's foot. "Your gift is best of all, good fellow," said he. "You may choose your own reward. Will you take land? Or servants? Or gold?"

"I thank you, good king," said Sir Cleges. "But I ask only the right to pay twelve strokes of my staff where I wish."

When King Uther heard this, he grew angry. "That is no boon to ask on Christmas Day!" said he.

But Sir Cleges would have no other gift. So the king gave a grumble and agreed, for he would not go back on his word.

At once Sir Cleges turned aside and paid the king's proud steward four of the twelve strokes across his shoulders. Then he went out to pay the usher his four, and the porter at the gate four more.

And, lo! When the good knight returned to the great hall, a minstrel was singing an old song of the deeds of the famous Sir Cleges!

"A brave tale!" King Uther exclaimed when the song had been sung. "But what of stouthearted Sir Cleges now? Is he alive or in heaven? I have not seen him in many a year."

The minstrel did not know, nor the harper, nor the lords and ladies or other fine folk in the hall.

"Alas!" King Uther sighed. "Then I fear the good, brave knight is dead. Would God he were still among us!"

At that Sir Cleges came again to kneel before the king. "I thank you, sire," said he, "for the boon you granted me."

"Come," said the king, "tell us, fellow, why you took twelve strokes instead of good, rich land."

So Sir Cleges told of the three proud servants who had barred his way, and how each had made him promise to pay a third of the king's reward. The lords and ladies laughed to hear the tale, and King Uther laughed loudest of all.

"Ho!" said he. "They will not play such tricks soon again. I am glad to know such a clever fellow. Come, tell us your name, friend farmer."

"Indeed, sire, I am Sir Cleges," the good knight said, and he and his son bowed low.

"Sir Cleges!" the king shouted. "Praise God!"

And all the knights and their ladies cried, "Huzzah!"

That night, when Sir Cleges returned home to Dame Clarys, he rode a fine horse and his son rode another. Together they brought her the best news that could be.

King Uther had dubbed Sir Cleges the Christmas Knight, and made him lord of Cardiff Castle. There, each year at Christmas, he was to feast the homeless and hungry and poor in the king's own name.

And so, of course, the good knight and his wife and sons lived merrily ever after.

And twice as merrily at Christmastime.